A Perfect Day

LANE SMITH

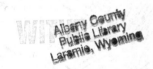
ROARING BROOK PRESS
NEW YORK

In memory of Bert

Feeder of bird
Feeder of squirrel

Published by Roaring Brook Press
Roaring Brook Press is a division of Holtzbrinck Publishing Holdings Limited
Partnership
175 Fifth Avenue, New York, New York 10010
mackids.com

Library of Congress Cataloging-in-Publication Data

Names: Smith, Lane, author, illustrator.
Title: A perfect day / Lane Smith.
Description: First edition. | New York : Roaring Brook Press, 2016. |
    Summary: "A perfect day means different things to different animals in
    Bert's backyard"—Provided by publisher.
Identifiers: LCCN 2016024231 | ISBN 9781626725362 (hardback)
Subjects: | CYAC: Animals—Fiction. | BISAC: JUVENILE FICTION /
    Animals / General. | JUVENILE FICTION / Humorous Stories. |
    JUVENILE FICTION / General.
Classification: LCC PZ7.S6538 Pe 2016 | DDC [E]—dc23
LC record available at https://lccn.loc.gov/2016024231

Our books may be purchased in bulk for promotional, educational,
or business use. Please contact your local bookseller or the
Macmillan Corporate and Premium Sales Department at (800) 221-7945 ext.
5442 or by e-mail at MacmillanSpecialMarkets@macmillan.com.

First edition 2017
Book design by Molly Leach
Printed in China by RR Donnelley Asia Printing Solutions Ltd., Dongguan City,
Guangdong Province

10 9 8 7 6 5 4 3 2 1

The warmth of the sun . . .

felt good on Cat's back.

Cat liked to be in
the flower bed where
the daffodils grew.

It was a perfect day for Cat.

The cool of the water was what Dog liked best.

When it was hot, Dog sat in the wading pool that his friend Bert filled for him.

It was a perfect day for Dog.

Birdseed.

Bert topped off the
bird feeder with it.

It was a perfect day for Chickadee.

Squirrel went up
the pole.

Squirrel went
down the pole.

Squirrel could not
get to the seed.

Bert dropped a corncob onto the grass.

It was a perfect day for Squirrel.

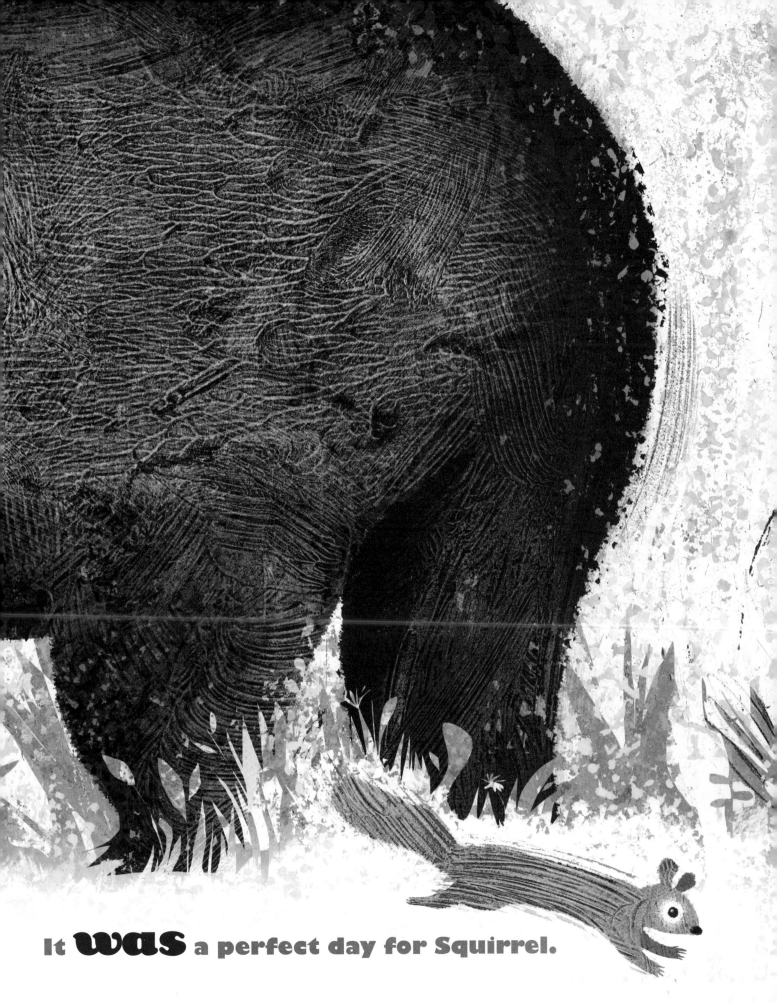

It **was** a perfect day for Squirrel.

It **was** a perfect day for Chickadee.

It **was** a perfect day for Dog.

It **was** a perfect day for Cat.

The warmth of the sun.
The cool of the water.
A belly full of corn and seed.
A flower bed for a nap.

It was a perfect day for Bear.